Marty's

Crazy Adventures

School Daze

by Christy Harrison

illustrated by Avoltha

To Tony, Briggs, and Jersey whom
I love so much

For Troy and Kiley that touched my life
in special ways

This book is a work of fiction. No part of this publication may be reproduced, stored in a retrieval system, or transmitted in any form or by any means, electronic, mechanical, photocopying, recording, or otherwise without written permission of the publisher.

ISBN-13: 978-1479195244
ISBN-10: 1479195243

Printed in the U.S.A.

TABLE OF CONTENTS

CHAPTER 1

GET UP!!!

"Marty, time to wake up," Mother said in a quiet voice. Marty rolled over and began talking in his sleep in a baby voice, "I don't want to go to school, Mommy." "Marty, get up out of bed so you can get ready for school," she nudged. Marty snoozed even louder.

Mom shouted in his ear, "Marty, get up!!!"

Marty jumped up out of bed and threw on his clothes and began singing his favorite song (sung to the tune of "Money, Money, Money, Mon---ey!").

"Marty, Marty, Marty, Mar---ty!"

He ran downstairs like a flash of lightning and turned the T.V. on to watch his favorite show, *Galaxy Rangers*. Marty began to act out the fight scene he was watching by using his favorite laser gun. "Take that! Zap! Zap! Zap! Captain Marty takes no prisoners!"

"Marty! Breakfast!" his mother called.

Marty continued to fight with all his might as he leaped off of the couch and shot everything in sight. "No one will escape from Planet Zero!!! No one, I tell you!!!" Just then, his mother appeared in the doorway with his baby sister, Ruthie, on her hip. "You won't escape from MY clutches if you don't come eat your breakfast right now," she said sternly.

"You must learn how to control yourself."

Marty quickly gobbled down his oatmeal and grapes and headed for the bus stop.

Chapter 2

Bouncy Bus Ride

As Marty boarded the bus, he shouted, "Have no fear! Marty is here!" "Sit down, Marty," Mr. Brown, the bus driver, insisted. All the way to school, Marty bounced like a ping pong ball up and down in his seat.

As he stepped off of the bus, Mr. Brown warned him, "Marty, if you don't settle down and control yourself, you're gonna end up in a heap o' trouble!"

Chapter 3

Peepee Dancing

Class finally started, and Marty began to copy down his first math problem.

$$8 \times 7 = SNAP!!!$$

The lead on his pencil broke and rolled onto the floor.

"Mrs. Berry!" called Marty. "I need to sharpen my pencil!" "Go ahead, Marty," she answered. Marty danced over to the sharpener and began turning the crank. Whirr! Crunch! Squeek! Mrs. Berry rolled her eyes.

When Marty returned to his desk, he started talking to Joe about what he had seen on *Galaxy Rangers* that morning. "It was awesome! Captain Courage shot a lazerbeam right through the Master of Disaster! Pew! Pew!"

Joe suddenly felt Mrs. Berry's eyes burning a hole right through them. "Marty, that's enough! How many problems have you done?" she asked. "Uh, zero times seven," Marty answered. "It looks like you'll be missing some recess," said Mrs. Berry.

Marty raised his hand up in the air. "Yes,
Marty?" Mrs. Berry asked with a glare. "Can
I go to the bathroom?" Marty questioned
while starting his pee-pee dance. "Can you
not control yourself for 5 minutes?!!" Mrs.
Berry asked with a raised voice.

Chapter 4

YAY, CHEESE FRIES!

Later that day during lunch, Marty opened

up his *Galaxy Rangers* lunch bag to see that

his mom had packed him a PB&J, chips,

apple, and fruit juice. Marty glanced around

and saw that Joe was unpacking his lunch.

Joe reached in and pulled out a plastic

container and lifted the lid to reveal...........

CHEESE FRIES!!!!!!!!!

Since cheese fries are Marty's FAVORITE food, the very smell made his mouth begin to water with anticipation.

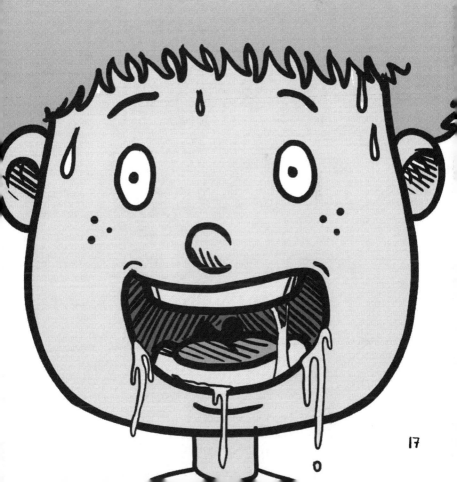

"Oh, I forgot to buy some milk," said Joe
as he got up from the table. Marty's brain
began to kick into overdrive. "I wonder if
Joe will notice if some of his cheese fries are
gone when he gets back."

Before he knew it, he had gobbled down

almost half of them.

When Joe returned, Marty looked at him with cheese sauce oozing out of the corners of his mouth.

"I'm sworwy. I houldn't hel ma sel," he said with his mouth full. "Marty! You could've waited and asked! I would've shared with you!" Joe said.

Chapter 5

Cutter, Cutter, Peanut Butter!

After lunch, it was time for recess. By the time Marty sat out for 10 minutes, the line for the slide was a mile long. Marty saw Alex near the front of the line and began to think about how he could get ahead without waiting.

23

He walked up to Alex and started telling him about *Galaxy Rangers*. Before his friends knew it, Marty had weaseled his way up the slide and cut.

"Marty! You cutted!" yelled Megan. "Sorry!
I couldn't help myself! The Master of Disaster
strikes again!" he shouted as he flew down
the slide.

25

Next, Marty decided to play four square. He made it all the way to the third square and got out.

He slammed the ball down in anger as hard as he could, and the ball went soaring through the air.

Breet! Breet!

The whistle blew, and Marty could see Mrs. Berry waving at him to come to her. Once again, Marty heard the word.................. "self-control."

"Self-control, self-control...yes, I need more of it. But how do I get it?" he thought.

Chapter 6

Paybacks!

Marty shoved his way in line as everyone

was leaving recess. As they all entered the

building, Marty began to rap his own "self-

control" song. And as we all know, teachers

want it to be quiet in the hallway as you travel from class to class. "Self-control, self-control, gotta listen to my heart, gotta do what is smart!" Marty rapped and tried to beat box in between, but he only ended up spitting on the people around him. "Shhhh!" Mrs. Berry scolded.

During P.E., the class was going to play dodgeball. "Oh yeah!!! Prepare to be clobbered, people!!!" Marty yelled. Balls were flying in every direction. Slam! Bam! Wham!

Marty was doing great! However, just
then, a stray ball came whizzing by out of
no where. Oof! It hit Marty right in the
stomach. "Yes!!! You're out, Marty! That's
for cutting in line on the slide!" shouted
Megan.

"No way! I can't get out by a girl!!!" Marty
yelled. "I won't go I tell you! You're goin'
down! Down to the ground!"

Just then, the whistle blew. Breet! Breet!

"Marty, you're out!" Mr. West, the P.E.

teacher, said sternly.

"Take a deep breath and sit down on the
side," Mr. West instructed. Marty held his
breath as he walked over to the sidelines and
sat down. This is something he often did to
try and calm himself.

After a minute passed, Marty began to turn

a little red. "You can let it out now, Marty,"

Mr. West said. Marty let out all of his hot

air. In doing so, he fell back onto the floor.

"Whew!" he said in relief. "Sometimes

we need to just cool off and think a minute

before we lose control," Mr. West explained.

Chapter 7

Explosion!!!

That afternoon, the bell rang, and it was time to run and catch the bus. "Whoo hoo!" Marty shouted. As he boarded the bus, he yelled, "Have no fear! Marty is here!" "Sit down, Marty," Mr. Brown said with disgust.

As Marty approached the back of the bus, he heard a familiar tune.

" ... sittin' in a tree
K-I-S-S-I-N-G!
First comes love,
Then comes marriage,
Here comes
Marty with a
baby carriage!"

39

The children squealed with delight. Just then, Marty put two and two together. The song they were singing was about Megan and HIM!!! Marty felt his face getting hot, and his body begin to shake with fury. He looked like a volcano about to erupt.

"He's gonna blow!!!" yelled a boy from the back of the bus. And blow he did.

That's it! I can't take it anymore! I'm eight years old! Everywhere I turn... trouble... trouble... TROUBLE!!!

Probs on the bus, probs at school, probs in Math, probs at lunch,

I LOVE CHEESE FRIES!, probs on the slide, probs in P.E. and here I am on the bus again with more PROBS!!!

What's a guy gotta do?!!!

Marty continued ranting nonstop for the next several blocks. The other kids on the bus fell silent as the bus driver finally screeched to a halt in front of Marty's house.

"Enough!" Mr. Brown shouted. "Hold your breath, Marty, and get off this bus!" Marty took a deep breath and held it all in. Silence. "Boy, he's lost it," whispered a girl with pigtails.

Chapter 8

Let it out!!!

As Marty made his way up the front steps,

he began to shake and turn blue in the face.

Still holding his breath, he opened the door

to his room and saw his mother.

"Son, are you o.k.?" she asked when she saw his condition. "Oh my word! Are you holding your breath?" Marty was shaking from head to toe. "Let it out! Let it out!" she screamed.

Marty released so much air that he flew backward into the wall. This caused a jolt that knocked over a container of legos off his bookshelf and onto his head.

"Marty, did you have a rough day at school?" his mother asked. "Yes," Marty mumbled from under the empty box that was on his head. "I messed up."

MARTY, YOU'VE GOT TO LEARN SOME SELF-CONTROL. HOLDING YOUR BREATH WON'T WORK UNTIL YOU THINK ABOUT THE RIGHT THING TO DO WHILE YOU'RE HOLDING IT. SOME TIMES WE MIGHT WANT TO DO THINGS THAT MAY NOT BE GOOD FOR US OR OTHERS. WE NEED TO LEARN TO MAKE GOOD CHOICES AND CONTROL OUR FEELINGS. UNDERSTAND?

"Yes, ma'am," Marty said as he stood up from the pile of legos. "Tomorrow is a new day! I will show self-control! I will conquer the universe!" he proclaimed. "Marty, how 'bout you start by conquering this room. It's a mess! Then, you can watch Galaxy Rangers."

"Yay, cheese fries!!!" he yelled as he soared

onto his bed. His mother gave Marty the eye.

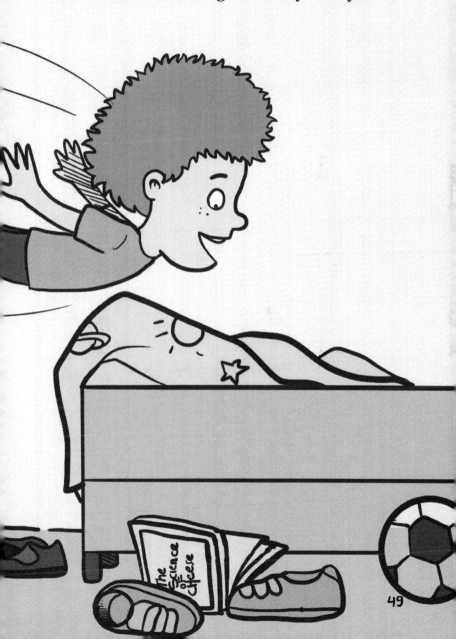

Just then, Ruthie appeared in the doorway with her face covered in her mom's favorite cherry red lipstick. "Ruthie, what have you done?!" her mother yelled.

"Mom, just hold your breath," said Marty
with a smile.

Similes

a comparison using "like" or "as"

pg. 5 - He ran downstairs <u>like a flash of lightning</u> and turned the T.V. on to watch his favorite show, "Galaxy Rangers."

pg. 10 - All the way to school, Marty bounced <u>like a ping pong ball</u> up and down in his seat.

pg. 41 - He looked <u>like a volcano</u> about to erupt.

Now you try one!

Marty moved as slow as _____

(Think of something that is always slow.)

as he picked up all of his legos.

About the Author

Christy Harrison loves kids and began working and teaching them at her local church when she was only twelve years old. In 1997, she received her degree in elementary education with a specialization in English. She and her husband have been children's pastors together for 22 years. Along with being an elementary teacher, Christy also enjoys leading her children's choir and worship team. She and Marty (the puppet) have entertained kids in schools, churches, and camps in the Central U.S. over the last twenty years. "It never gets old because I never know what Marty's going to do or say, which is sometimes scary," she says. Christy lives in Springdale, Arkansas, with her husband, Tony, and two kids, Briggs and Jersey.